6/07

Abigail Adams

First Lady of the American Revolution

written by **Patricia Lakin**

illustrated by

Bob Dacey and Debra Bandelin

Ready-to-Read •Aladdin
New York   London   Toronto   Sydney

This book is dedicated to you, a future voter! —P. L.

To Anna, Jennifer, Caroline, and Peter,
with love —B. D. & D. B.

❧

ALADDIN PAPERBACKS

An imprint of Simon & Schuster Children's Publishing Division

1230 Avenue of the Americas, New York, NY 10020

Text copyright © 2006 by Patricia Lakin

Illustrations copyright © 2006 by Bob Dacey and Debra Bandelin

All rights reserved, including the right of reproduction in whole or in part in any form.

READY-TO-READ is a registered trademark of Simon & Schuster, Inc.

ALADDIN PAPERBACKS and colophon are trademarks of Simon & Schuster, Inc.

Designed by Lisa Vega

The text of this book was set in CenturyOldst BT.

Manufactured in the United States of America

First Aladdin Paperbacks edition July 2006

2   4   6   8   10   9   7   5   3   1

Library of Congress Cataloging-in-Publication Data

Lakin, Patricia, 1944–

Abigail Adams : first lady of the American Revolution / by Patricia Lakin ;

illustrated by Bob Dacey and Debra Bandelin.—1st Aladdin Paperbacks ed.

p. cm.—(Ready-to-read stories of famous Americans)

ISBN-13: 978-0-689-87032-3 (pbk.)

ISBN-10: 0-689-87032-9 (pbk.)

ISBN-13: 978-0-689-87033-0 (lib.)

ISBN-10: 0-689-87033-7 (lib.)

1. Adams, Abigail, 1744–1818—Juvenile literature. 2. Presidents' spouses—United States—

Biography—Juvenile literature. 3. United States—History—Revolution, 1775–1783—

Juvenile literature. I. Dacey, Bob, ill. II. Bandelin, Debra, ill. III. Title. IV. Series.

E322.1.A38L35 2006

973.4'4'092—dc22

2005007955

CHAPTER 1
ABIGAIL'S EARLY YEARS

Abigail Adams lived at a time in America when women were expected to be wives and mothers—nothing more. But Abigail *was* far more! She helped shape the early history of the United States, influenced two of our nation's presidents, managed the family farm almost single-handedly, and became a clever businesswoman.

Abigail was the second child of Reverend William and Elizabeth Smith. She was born on November 11, 1744. The Smith family lived in a small cottage in Weymouth, Massachusetts, one of the thirteen British colonies that would soon become the United States of America.

Colonial girls did not attend school. Their mothers taught them only what they needed to know to become good wives and mothers. Abigail's mother taught Abigail and her two sisters how to cook, clean, sew, weave, make medicines from herbs, and raise vegetables. But Mrs. Smith taught Abigail something more.

As the minister's wife, Mrs. Smith reached out to those who attended her husband's church. Abigail often went with Mrs. Smith when she cared for the sick and helped the elderly and the needy. Mrs. Smith's concern for others in the community made a great impression on young Abigail.

But her father's unusual views on women's education also had a great impact. Reverend Smith encouraged all three of his daughters, Mary, Abigail, and Elizabeth, to value education and to read to their hearts' content.

Abigail loved to sit by the fireplace and read the books from her father's home library. She delighted in them all, whether they were Greek myths, the poetry of Alexander Pope, or the plays of William Shakespeare.

Abigail also began writing letters to friends. She wrote of her thoughts, ideas, and wishes. It was a hobby that would last throughout her lifetime.

Mrs. Smith worried that Abigail's strong desire to learn was not a good thing. She felt that Abigail was far too stubborn and outspoken in her opinions. Those qualities were not thought to be ladylike. Luckily for Abigail, her father and grandmother defended her bright mind and her independent streak. Her grandmother often said, "Wild colts make the best horses."

CHAPTER 2
ABIGAIL'S BEST FRIEND

Abigail was a beautiful, slender, fair-skinned young woman. Her strong opinions, her love for learning, and her curiosity did not stop young men from being attracted to her. One was a young lawyer, John Adams. He was ten years older than Abigail and came from nearby Braintree. Short, stout John Adams was a friend of Mary, Abigail's older sister.

Slowly, after several years and many visits to the Smith home, John and Abigail realized that they were very much alike. They both had keen minds, firm views, and enjoyed sharing their ideas. Abigail and John became best friends and fell deeply in love.

On October 25, 1764, just weeks before her twentieth birthday, Abigail Smith married John Adams. They moved to his farm in nearby Braintree. For the first year of their marriage, life was just as Abigail might have expected. She cared for her new home and husband. She bade him good-bye when he rode off on horseback to the Boston law courts. She visited her family in Weymouth when the roads were not snow covered or mud filled. She kept up her passion for reading when time allowed, and she kept up her letter writing to friends.

In July of 1765, Abigail and John's first child was born. She was named Abigail, but called Nabby.

Abigail and John spent many evenings by the fire, discussing the latest news—the growing bad feeling between the colonists and Britain.

Far from their cottage, across the Atlantic Ocean, the British king George III had finished fighting the seven-year French and Indian War. King George III began looking to the colonies for ways to replace the money he'd spent on that war.

In 1765 the British government created the Stamp Act. It stated that a stamp had to be purchased for all materials and documents printed in the colonies. That included all newspapers, marriage licenses, death certificates, deeds for buying and selling property, and even decks of playing cards.

The Stamp Act was a tax. The money collected from the stamps went back to Britain and gave no benefit to the colonies.

The chain of events caused by this Stamp Act changed the lives of Abigail and John Adams.

CHAPTER 3
TAXES! TAXES! TAXES!

Lawyers like John Adams were especially outraged by the Stamp Act. They couldn't do business without buying those stamps. The courts were shut down. Law offices, including John's, closed. But Abigail and John were not silent. They discussed how to oppose the actions of the king.

John began spending more and
more time away from home. He met
with other colonists, among them John
Hancock, Benjamin Franklin, and his
cousin Sam Adams. They urged people
to ignore the Stamp Act.

Abigail didn't mind John's absences.
She saw that their larger community—
the Massachusetts colony—needed
John's help.

One year after it was enacted, the Stamp Act was repealed. But stricter laws took its place.

In 1773, Britain passed the Tea Act. That law continued to tax the tea coming to the colonies, but from then on the colonists could buy their tea only from the company and merchants chosen by the British.

When three ships carrying tea sailed into Boston Harbor, Abigail, John, and many other colonists didn't want them to unload. That way no taxes would be due. But the British insisted on payment whether the tea was unloaded or not.

Angry colonists planned a way to protest. On the night of December 16, 1773, men dressed as Mohawks crept onto the ships and dumped the crates of tea into Boston Harbor.

Abigail and John thought that event, called the Boston Tea Party, was necessary. Britain had to see how furious the colonists were about being taxed without having a say in the matter.

Several months after the Boston Tea Party, John came to Abigail with exciting news. John, Ben Franklin, and others had been chosen to be part of a new group called the Continental Congress. It included men from all thirteen colonies. They would meet in Philadelphia to work out peaceful agreements with Britain on the things that were angering the colonists.

John would be far from home now, and stay away for longer periods of time. Besides their first child, Nabby, Abigail and John had three more children: John Quincy, Charles, and Thomas. (Their daughter Susanna died in 1770 at the age of two.) But Abigail saw that their much larger community—the thirteen colonies—needed John's help.

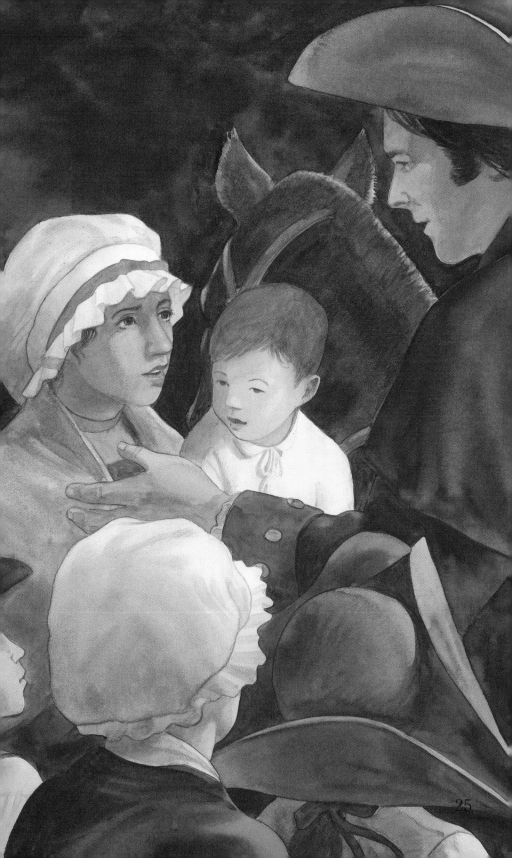

CHAPTER 4
WAR!

By the spring of 1775, John had been in Philadelphia for nine months. Abigail, like other colonists, feared war between the colonies and Britain would start at any moment. She missed John all the more.

Then, in April, Abigail heard the news. The war had begun with a battle at Lexington and Concord. The British soldiers, or redcoats, snuck toward Lexington hoping to attack. But Paul Revere and William Dawes warned the colonists ahead of time. The redcoats faced the Minutemen of Massachusetts.

War had broken out at Lexington and Concord. Then, on June 17, in Braintree, Abigail heard cannons firing and saw smoke billowing from Boston. It was the battle of Bunker Hill. She wrote John that with "... the constant roar of the cannon ... we can not Eat, Drink or Sleep."

But that letter took a while to reach John. Like all mail, it traveled only as fast as a person on horseback could go. And Abigail couldn't count on John's letters to arrive in time to help her make family decisions. More and more, Abigail had to trust her own judgment.

She chose where and how to educate her children. She clung to her belief in equal education for boys and girls. So daughter Nabby learned Latin alongside her brothers. Abigail made decisions about the family money and who to hire to help with their farm. And she decided to buy nearby pieces of land when they came up for sale.

Her letters to John, filled with family news, eased his homesickness. They also offered strong opinions, especially her wishes for a stronger women's role in their new country. In March of 1776, she wrote, "I desire you would Remember the Ladies. . . . Do not put such unlimited power into the hands of the Husbands."

Through her letters she became John's eyes and ears. They were filled with what she had seen and heard at home. They gave John the fuel he needed to change the views of some Congress members. Some thought the fights in and around Boston were the work of a few "troublemakers." Her letters proved otherwise. John even quoted from one in a speech he gave.

Finally the representatives of the Continental Congress agreed. All thirteen colonies decided to break from British rule. On July 4, 1776, the group approved a document called the Declaration of Independence. And like her beloved country, Abigail was showing her own growing independence as well.

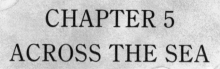

CHAPTER 5
ACROSS THE SEA

Throughout 1777, General George Washington and others won major battles. France joined with the colonists to fight the British.

That good news brought Abigail heartbreaking news as well. John had been asked to sail to France to join Benjamin Franklin there.

Their job was to convince France to trade directly with the colonists. She hated having John so far away, but Abigail saw that their much larger community— America—needed John's help. And Abigail made another sacrifice: She asked that their son John Quincy go to France too. Learning French and traveling would be an excellent education for him.

Abigail and the rest of her children couldn't join John and John Quincy. They didn't have the money. Abigail couldn't leave the farm unattended. And storms, and attacking British ships, made sea travel dangerous.

On February 13, 1778, a sad and
worried Abigail said good-bye to John and
ten-year-old John Quincy.

Once again Abigail was determined
to be John's hands, eyes, and ears. She
worked the farm. She cared for their
family. And she wrote him long letters
with news of home.

John and John Quincy returned home
after a year and a half. But John was soon
sent back to France, this time as head of
the American group. Abigail agreed that
their younger son Charles should travel
to France with John and John Quincy. The
three left in November of 1779.

By now, after being married for fifteen years, Abigail knew that John would spend his life in politics. She also knew that politicians didn't make much money. So Abigail found ways to plan for their later years. She had John send her goods from France, like silk hankies and fine glassware, which she sold. She put some of their money into businesses, and she bought and sold land. All the while, she cared for their family and farm.

In France, John was helping write
the peace treaty between America and
Britain. By January of 1784 all sides
agreed that the American Revolutionary
War was over.

Finally, after five long years away from John, forty-year-old Abigail, along with eighteen-year-old Nabby, crossed the Atlantic Ocean.

By August of 1784, Abigail and John were together once more. Home was not a cottage in Braintree. It was a thirty-room mansion in Paris, France, that John had rented. After one year there, John got exciting news. He'd been chosen as the first American ambassador to Britain.

In June of 1785, almost nine years after America declared war against King George III, Abigail was to meet that very same king.

Meeting King George III was just one of Abigail's pleasures in Britain. She also enjoyed seeing the plays of Shakespeare—the very ones she'd read as a girl.

CHAPTER 6
JOHN'S FIRST LADY

By 1788, after four years away, Abigail felt it was time to come home. She missed her grown children and little grandchildren. She wrote, ". . . I do not regret that I made this excursion since it has only more attached me to America."

Soon after they landed in Boston, a new government document took effect. It was the United States Constitution and called for a president and vice president.

George Washington was elected president and John Adams was elected vice president.

Once again Abigail saw that the far greater community—the United States of America—needed John's help. Once more she left Braintree and moved with John to the nation's first capital, New York City.

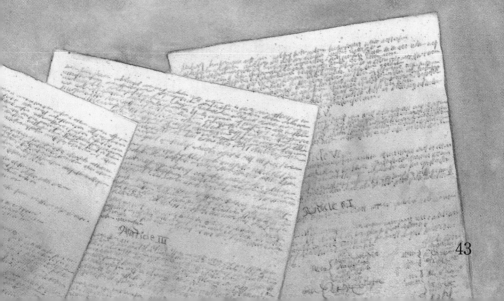

When George Washington's second term ended, John Adams was elected president. He was sworn in on March 4, 1797, in the nation's new capital, Philadelphia. Abigail, the new "First Lady," was in Braintree, caring for John's dying mother. John wrote her, "I never wanted your Advice and assistance more in my Life." Finally, in April, she joined John.

During his presidency the capital moved again, to an area named for George Washington.

John and Abigail moved into the still-unfinished President's House, known today as the White House. Abigail had to hang her laundry inside the house, since the grounds were muddy fields, like the rest of Washington, D.C.

John served for only one term. In 1801, they went home to Massachusetts for good.

Abigail cared for her family, her grandchildren, her garden, and of course, John. She saw their oldest son, John Quincy, follow in his father's political footsteps. But she never saw him take the oath of office as the sixth president of the United States. Abigail Adams died at home on October 28, 1818. She was almost seventy-four.

Abigail Adams was swept into the political events of the day. During her life she was guided by three loves: her love for learning, her love for her family, and her love for her country. Those—along with her greatest love, John Adams—helped her to shape the early history of the United States.

Abigail Adams Time Line

1744	Abigail is born on November 11 in Weymouth, Massachusetts.
1764	Abigail marries John on October 25.
1765	First child, Abigail, or "Nabby," is born on July 14.
1767	First son, John Quincy, is born on July 11.
1770	Second daughter, Susanna, dies at age two.
	Second son, Charles, is born on May 29.
1772	Third son, Thomas, is born on September 15.
1774	Abigail sees John off to Philadelphia for the Continental Congress.
1775	Abigail is alone with the children when the Revolutionary War starts on April 19.
1778	John and John Quincy sail for France in February.
1779	John and John Quincy return in August. They sail off again with Charles in November.
1782	Abigail welcomes Charles home in January.
1784	With the Revolutionary War now officially over, Abigail and Nabby sail for France on June 20.
1785–1787	Abigail and John, now first American ambassador to Britain, live in London.
1788	Abigail and John return to Boston on June 17.
1789	John is elected the country's first vice president.
1797	Abigail becomes First Lady in March after John is elected president.
1801	Abigail and John return to private life in March.
1818	Abigail dies at home on October 28.

W9-CFS-981

NUMBER MYSTERIES

Author :	Cyril Hayes
	Dympna Hayes
Art Director:	Rick Rowden
Illustrators:	Peggy McEwen
	Shane Doyle
	Rick Rowden
	Jodi Shuster

ISBN 0-88625-145-1

CHP BOOKS

3312 Mainway, Burlington, Ontario L7M 1A7, Canada
2045 Niagara Falls Blvd., Unit 14, Niagara Falls, NY 14304, U.S.A.

COUNTING AND SEQUENCING GAMES

Place 10 coins like this:

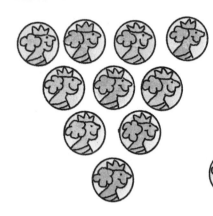

Now move only 3 coins to get this:

SHOVEL IT UP

Make this shovel by using four matchsticks. Place the penny in the spot shown on diagram A. Now, using only two moves of the matchsticks, trap the penny inside the shovel. HINT: The shovel can face any way you like.

MOON GAME

Toss a penny: Heads, move 1 space; tails, move 2.

START

Rocket launch, move back one space

Crater lake, miss a turn

Moon Taxi, jump 2 spaces

Approaching Warp Factor 5, toss again

Moon Canyon- miss a turn

Moon Base Alpha II

FINISH

DID YOU KNOW?

If you were born one billion hours ago, you would be a caveman.

QUICK QUIZ

How many Tuesdays in a year?

DAYS

3

EQUAL EXPENSES

Dave rents a car to drive to a city 100 kilometers away. He stops halfway and picks up Pam, who rides the last 50 kilometers with him.

Returning in the evening with Pam, Dave drops her where he picked her up, then drives on to his starting point where he is charged $24 for car rental.

Dave and Pam want to share the cost so each pays for their fair share. How much should each one pay?

STAR WONDER

Write down the missing numbers so that the sum of the numbers in each straight line equals the total in the middle. Redraw the diagram in your notebook.

ALL SQUARED UP

Place twenty-four sticks so that they form nine squares. Can you take away eight sticks, leaving only two squares?

THE CLIMBING CATERPILLAR

One morning a caterpillar started climbing a tree trunk 13 m long. Each day he climbed 3 m, and each night he slipped back 2 m. How many days did it take him to reach the top?

DINNER DATES

Every week 22 friends dine around a circular table. At each new meal, every diner tries to sit between 2 new friends. So, if Mary sits between Jane and Jeff this week, she will never sit next to Jane or Jeff again. After how many weeks will each guest have sat exactly once beside every other guest?

HINT: It helps if you draw a picture of the table and 22 guests.

HUNGRY RABBITS

Use 2 straws or pencils to make a fence that separates all the rabbits from the carrots.

QUICK QUIZ

If the day before yesterday was Sunday, what is the day after tomorrow?

DID YOU KNOW?

One billion pennies laid end to end would stretch halfway around the world.

MIND READING

Think of a number between 1 and 31. Point to the cards on which the number appears. Add together the first number on each of those cards. What did you discover?

Make a set of cards like these. Ask your friend to point to the cards that have the day of the month his or her birthday is on. All you do is add up the first number on each of these cards and "TA DA" you can tell them what day of the month they were born on.

16	17	18	19
20	21	22	23
24	25	26	27
28	29	30	31

8	9	10	11
12	13	14	15
24	25	26	27
28	29	30	31

2	3	6	7
10	11	14	15
18	19	22	23
26	27	30	31

1	3	5	7
9	11	13	15
17	19	21	23
25	27	29	31

4	5	6	7
12	13	14	15
20	21	22	23
28	29	30	31

CRACKING SECRET CODES

"Two wrongs don't make a right."

See if you can find a code so that these two "wrongs" add up to "right."

wrong Hint: o=0 n=8
<u>wrong</u>   g=1 i=4
right

How about this one?

Xmas   Hint: a=8   l=0
mail   s=4   e=9
<u>+early</u>   i=6
please

QUICK QUIZ

Three boys ate 3 apples in 3 minutes. At that rate, how long would it take 8 boys to eat 8 apples?

	11	14	1
13		7	12
3		9	6
	5	4	15

MAGIC SQUARE

Copy down this square and the numbers on a piece of paper. Then fill in the missing numbers so that the numbers in each row and column add up to 34.

SMARTYPANTS

Here's a trick that will stump your friends every time. Ask one of your friends to pick 2 numbers between 1 and 9 but not to tell you. Tell him to take either number, multiply it by 5, then add 7 and double the sum. Now ask him to add the other secret number and subtract 14. When he tells you the result, each digit will be a number he originally thought of.

HUNGRY HENS

If 73 hens lay 73 dozen eggs in 73 days, and if 37 hens eat 37 kilograms of wheat in 37 days, what weight of wheat corresponds to 1 dozen eggs?

NUMBER DETECTIVE

Can you find the numbers hiding in these pictures?

WHAT IS YOUR REACTION TIME?

Your reaction time is the time it takes you to react to something. A goalie's reaction time is the time between seeing the ball and making the save. A goalie must have a reaction time which is a small fraction of a second.

Here's how to measure your reaction time.

[graph- Reaction time in seconds/ Distance ruler falls in centimeters/ Reaction time vs Distance Ruler Falls]

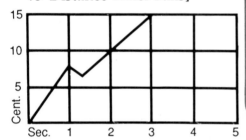

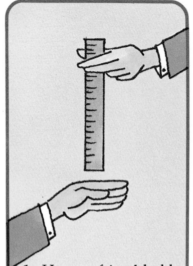

1. Have a friend hold a centimeter ruler with the 0 cm mark between your thumb and forefinger.

2. When your friend releases the ruler grab it as quickly as you can.

3. Then record the distance the ruler fell before you grabbed it.

4. Read your reaction time from the graph.

5. Repeat the experiment several times to see if your reaction time speeds up.

MONICA'S MONEY

Monica spent all of her money in 5 stores. In each store she spent $1 more than half of what she had when she came in.

How much did Monica have when she entered the first store?

12

CAN YOU MAKE A "T" OUT OF A TEAHOUSE?

Trace and cut out the teahouse tangram below.

Then rearrange the pieces so that they form a "T."

HINT: Make the tangram out of cardboard.

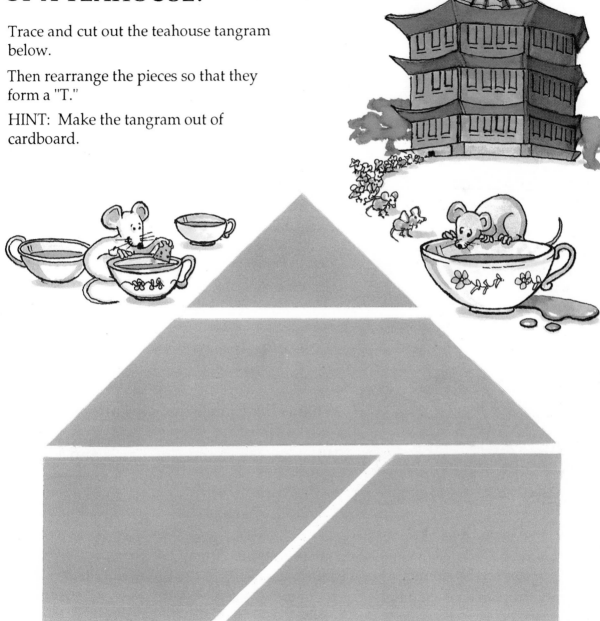

BOYS AND GIRLS

When a baby is born, the chance that it is a boy is the same as the chance that it is a girl.

In a family with 4 children:

The chances that all 4 children are boys are: 1 chance in 16

The chances of 3 boys and 1 girl are: 1 chance in 4

The chances of 2 boys and 2 girls are: 3 chances in 8

What is the chance that all 4 are girls?

What are the chances of 3 girls and 1 boy?

DID YOU KNOW?

Every day your heart does enough work to raise a train engine 1 meter off the ground. Over a lifetime, it will beat more than three billion times. That's better than any man-made machine.

14

A CHINESE TANGRAM

Trace this tangram; then cut out each piece.

Now arrange the pieces to make these shapes. You will need all the pieces for each shape.

HINT: Make your pieces out of cardboard.

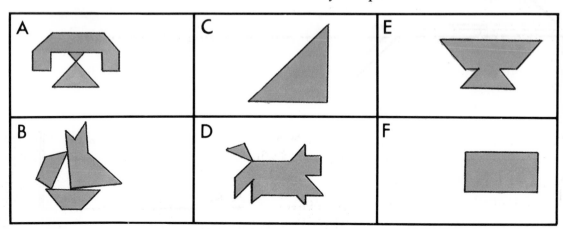

A

B

C

D

E

F

THE PILGRIM FATHERS

Riddle: Where did the Pilgrim Fathers stand when they landed on Plymouth Rock?
1. Begin at the START.
2. Then move along a path to a rock with a larger number.
3. Keep moving to a rock with a larger number until you reach the FINISH.

I 110 011	R 110 100	F 110 110	B 110 101	111 101 FINISH
E 110 010	A 101 001	E 110 111	E 111 001	T 111 011
H 110 000	T 101111	W 101 110	C 111 000	G 111 010
O 100 111	N 101 100	D 100 010	K 111 011	H 111 100
100 101 START	G 101 101	M 100 110	N 110 001	P 111 110

To answer the riddle: Write the letters in your path in order. The first 2 letters are: ON

☐ ☐   ☐ ☐ ☐ ☐ ☐   ☐ ☐ ☐ ☐

DID YOU KNOW?
To make one billion dollars you would have to earn $1,000 every hour for about 115 years.

16

HOW TALL WILL YOU GROW?

FIND YOUR GROWTH FACTOR IN THIS TABLE:

AGE	BOYS	GIRLS
8	1.39	1.28
9	1.33	1.23
10	1.28	1.19
11	1.23	1.14
12	1.19	1.07
13	1.15	1.03

There is no way to figure out exactly how tall you will be when you finish growing. By using growth factors, we can estimate how tall you will be.

Multiply your height by your growth factor. Your answer is an estimate of how tall you will be as an adult.

You'll have to wait a few years to find out how good your estimate is.

QUICK QUIZ

Guess how many children are in the world.

10,000,000?
100,000,000?
1,000,000,000?

17

TRAVELING TRAINS

Two trains chug up and down the tracks between 2 towns. They have the same constant speeds: a high speed going uphill and a low speed going downhill.

The first train leaves town A as the second train leaves town B. They pass each other 7 miles from town A; they stop 4 minutes each at their destinations; they start back and pass each other the second time at 9 miles from town A. What is the distance between the towns?

"TOWN A"

BICYCLING BUDDIES

Craig and Tim want to find out who's the fastest cyclist, but they only have one bike. On a level road Craig races from kilometer 1 to kilometer 12, Tim timing him from the backseat. On the same road Tim races from kilometer 12 to kilometer 24, with Craig on the back seat. Craig wins easily. Is it because he rides faster, weighs more, or because of some other reason?

"TOWN B"

THE BIG CHEESE BALL

The Mouseville's Annual Charity Cheese Ball was attended by 1,200 mice who paid a total of $24,000. The father mice paid $100 a ticket, the mother mice paid $40 a ticket and the children were admitted for $2 each.

How many fathers, mothers and children attended?

PUPPIE PALS

Daisy loves to walk. Her constant speed is 6 km per hour.

Every day at noon she meets her pal Rover at a fire hydrant about halfway between their homes. Rover walks a little slower than Daisy: about 5.5 km per hour.

If both puppies reach the fire hydrant exactly at noon, how far are they from each other at 11:00 a.m.?

HEADS OR TOES

In a stable there are men and horses. In all, there are 22 heads and 72 feet. How many men and how many horses are in the stable?

HINT: 72 feet equal 36 pairs of feet.

20

TINY
TEENA

Tiny Teena, the trapeze artist, has a daring feat to perform before a live audience. On the way up the ladder, she starts to get a little stage fright and stops halfway up. If Tiny Teena starts on the middle rung, goes down 4 rungs, up 9 rungs, down 7 rungs, up 4 rungs, and up 11 more rungs to reach the top of the ladder, how many rungs are there on the ladder?

HINT: Number the middle rung as "O."

DINNER DILEMMA

Melanie is having dinner with Cam. She brought 5 dishes and Cam brought 3 dishes.

At the last minute Dave comes and eats with them. Dave pays $4 as his share. If all the dishes have the same value, how can the money be divided between Melanie and Cam?

CECIL'S CHAINS

Cecil owns 13 chains. Each chain has a central link interlocked with 2 other links. There is a total of 13x3=39 links, all closed.

Cecil wants to use all the small chains to make a closed chain of 39 links. He needs 4 minutes to cut open a link and 10 minutes to close it by soldering.

Cecil makes the big chain in 140 minutes. How does he do it?

TAXI TWINS

Rickie and Mickie compete in the annual taxi race, driving several times around a closed circuit. Rickie can drive the circuit in 25 minutes, but Mickie takes 30 minutes.

If the 2 drivers start at the same time, how long will it take Rickie to lap Mickie?

SILLY SEVENS

These 7s are so silly they don't know their proper arithmetical symbols.

$$7 \ 7 \ 7 \ 7 = 3$$
$$7 \ 7 \ 7 \ 7 = 8$$
$$7 \ 7 \ 7 \ 7 = 13$$
$$7 \ 7 \ 7 \ 7 = 15$$
$$7 \ 7 \ 7 \ 7 = 48$$
$$7 \ 7 \ 7 \ 7 = 56$$
$$7 \ 7 \ 7 \ 7 = 105$$

Please! Somebody show the silly 7s what their symbols should be!

PROFESSOR McMATH

Follow Professor McMath's instructions to see what happens.

Your answer is always 1,089 as long as you start with a number having first and last digits that differ by more than one.

Follow the steps above for each of these numbers: 265; 529; 700. Did you end up with 1,089 each time?

Try this trick on your friend. Tell your friend to pick a number. Then explain the steps but don't look at your friend's work. Then guess the answer 1,089 at the end. Watch your friend's surprise.

24

A MATH GENIUS

his story, it is said, took place in Germany in 1787. Karl Friedrich Gauss, then a boy of 0, began to show his genius for mathematics. Within a few short years, he showed imself to be one of the three greatest mathematicians of all time.

. Find the sum of the numbers from 1 ɔ 10 using Gauss's method. We have rouped the numbers for you.

1+2+3+4+5+6+7+8+9+10

Vhat is the sum of each pair?
Iow many pairs?

2. Use Gauss's method to find the sum of the numbers from 1 to 20.

3. What is the sum of the numbers from 1 to 19?

4. What is the sum of the numbers from 11 to 20?

MATH MAGIC

The day and month of your birth.

This chart shows the numbers of the months.

January	1	July	7
February	2	August	8
March	3	September	9
April	4	October	10
May	5	November	11
June	6	December	12

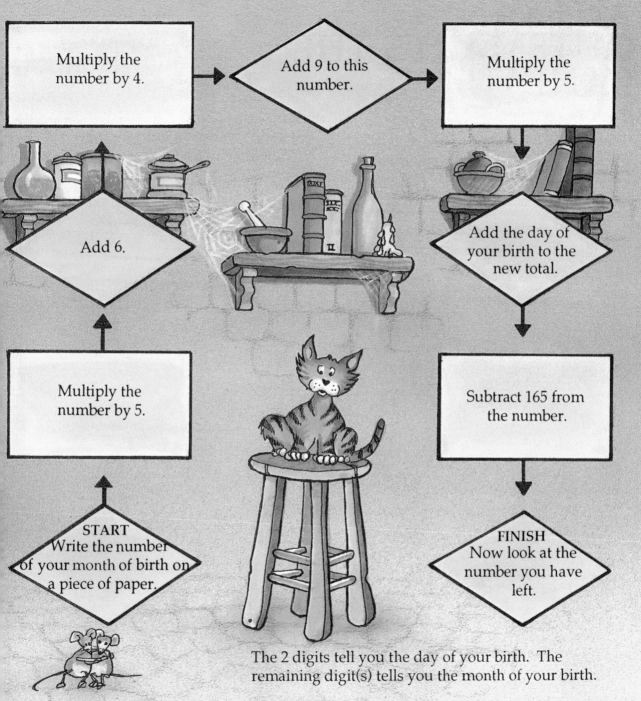

Multiply the number by 4.

Add 9 to this number.

Multiply the number by 5.

Add 6.

Add the day of your birth to the new total.

Multiply the number by 5.

Subtract 165 from the number.

START
Write the number of your month of birth on a piece of paper.

FINISH
Now look at the number you have left.

The 2 digits tell you the day of your birth. The remaining digit(s) tells you the month of your birth.

A TEXAN OUTSMARTS THE BANDITS

1 The story is told in the days of the Old West there was a gang of 6 bandits who held up the stagecoach from El Paso.

2 This was not an ordinary robbery. The stagecoach was carrying the bank reserves...a bagfull of gold nuggets!

3 The 6 bandits agreed to divide the nuggets into 6 equal shares.

4 But when they divided the nuggets into 6 equal piles, they found there was 1 left over.

They tried counting out 5 equal piles, but again there there was 1 left over.

There was also 1 left over when they tried to divide the nuggets into 4 equal piles.

Unable to share the nuggets equally, the men began to quarrel.

5 Suddenly, a Texan appeared on the scene.

"Listen, pardners, I'll solve your problem, but you pay me 1 gold nugget in advance!"

6 The bandits agreed. The Texan took the gold nugget and said as he mounted his horse,

"The remaining nuggets can now be divided equally among 6, 5, 4, 3, or 2 people!"

How many nuggets were in the bag that the bandits stole?

LETTERS FROM CAMP

1. Try to solve Bill's problem without looking at the answer.

2. Now try to solve his father's problem.

HAPPY CAMP
DEAR DAD
NO MON
NO FUN
YOUR SON
BILL

DEAR BILL
HOW SAD!
TOO BAD!
YOUR DAD.

DEAR DAD
HERE IS A PUZZLE FOR YOU.
EACH LETTER STANDS FOR A
DIFFERENT NUMBER BETWEEN
1 and 9. FIND THE NUMBER FOR
EACH LETTER WHICH MAKES THIS
A CORRECT ADDITION QUESTION.
HINT: M=1 O=0
D=7 Y=Z
SEND
+MORE
MONEY   BILL

DEAR BILL
THANK YOU FOR YOUR
INTERESTING PUZZLE. THE
ANSWER IS 9567
+1085
10 652
USE HINT S=1 Y=6
HERE IS ONE FOR YOU
P.S. SORRY BUT I'VE ALREADY
$50 I WOULD HAVE ENCLOSED
SEALED THE ENVELOPE
DAD

DID YOU KNOW?

Lord Kelvin proved that the coldest possible temperature is -273°C. This is called absolute zero.

QUICK QUESTION:

What is half of two divided by a half?

29

PAGE 2/3

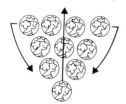

There are 52 Tuesdays in a year.

PAGE 4/5
EQUAL EXPENSES

Dave rode 200 kilometers and Pam 100 kilometers, for a total of 300 "passenger kilometers." Each passenger kilometer is worth 2400/300 = $0.08.
Dave should pay 200x.08 = $16.00 and Pam 100 x .08=$8.00.

STAR WONDER   ALL SQUARED UP

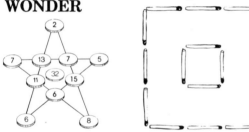

PAGE 6/7
It took the caterpillar 13 days.
HUNGRY RABBITS

30

DINNER DATES
Did this puzzle trap you? Each guest has 21 friends, so he/she can't sit beside 21 friends each week because eventually they would end up sitting next to 1 person twice. Take Mary as an example.

QUICK QUIZ
The day after tomorrow is Thursday.

PAGE 8/9
TWO WRONGS DON'T
MAKE A RIGHT

3,784
7,860

Problem with first one. 98,205
109,849

At the rate the boys are eating the apples, it takes 1 boy 3 minutes to eat 1 apple, so it would take 8 boys 3 minutes to eat 8 apples.

PAGE 10/11   A MAGIC SQUARE

8	1	14	1
13	2	7	12
3	16	9	6
10	5	4	15

SMARTYPANTS
Here's how it works. Let's say he thought of 3 and 7. He took 7 first and multiplied by 5. The result would be 35. Adding 7 to that makes 42. Doubling it makes 84. Adding the other number 3 makes it 87. When he subtracts 14, the final answer is 73 or 7 and 3.
As you can see, you are asking your friend to multiply the original number by 5 then 2 which is really 10. The adding 7, doubling it, and subtracting 14 is to confuse him. When the second number is added to 10 times the first one, naturally you get the two numbers he thought of.

NUMBER DETECTIVE
The numbers are: 5, 3+9

HUNGRY HENS

73 hens lay a total of 1 dozen eggs in 1 day, and 37 hens eat a total of 1 kilogram of wheat in 1 day. To get a dozen eggs you must feed 73 hens for 1 day. This requires 73/37 kilograms of wheat - a little less than 2 kg.

PAGE 12/13
MONICA'S MONEY

Monica entered each store with twice as much as the amount which is $1 more than she had when she left. Since she was broke when she left the fifth store, she entered it with: (0+1) x 2=$2

Likewise, she entered :

the fourth store with (2+1)x2=$6
the third store with (6+1)x2=$14
the second store with (14+1) x 2= $30
the first store with (30+1) x 2=$62

Monica started with $62.00

"T" OUT OF TEAHOUSE

PAGE 14/15
BOYS AND GIRLS

The chance that all 4 are girls is the same as the chance that all 4 are boys - 1 chance in 16.
The chances of 3 girls and 1 boy are -1 chance in 4.

PAGE 16/17
THE PILGRIM FATHERS
ON THEIR FEET

QUICK QUIZ - 1,000,000,000

PAGE 18/19
TRAVELING TRAINS

Since the trains arrive and depart from their home towns at the same times,
the problem is symmetrical. A distance from town A can be considered as if it were a distance from town B. Thus, we can add 7 miles from town A to 9 miles from town B to get the total distance: 16 miles.

BICYCLING BUDDIES

It is 11 kilometers from kilometer 1 to kilometer 12, but 12 kilometers from kilometer 12 to kilometer 24. Craig bicycled a shorter distance.

THE BIG CHEESE BALL

170 father mice, 140 mother mice, 900 children.

PAGE 20/21
PUPPIE PALS

They are 6 + 5.5 = 11.5 km from each other.

HEADS OR TOES

There are 72 feet altogether; 72 feet or 36 pairs of feet. There are 36 pairs of feet, but only 22 heads. This leaves 36-22=14, 14 pairs of feet left over.

So there have to be 14 horses, since horses have 2 pairs of feet each.

14 horses times 2 pairs of feet each are 28 pairs of feet.

36 pairs of feet less 28 pairs of feet leave 8 pairs of feet.

Each man has only 1 pair of feet, so there are 8 men.

14 horses + 8 men = 22 heads

TINY TEENA

Say Teena starts on rung "0." She goes down to rung 4 (-4) up to rung 5, down to rung -2, up to rung 2 and again up to 13. There are 2x13 +1 (the middle rung) = 27 rungs.

PAGE 22/23
DINNER DILEMMA

Since Dave paid $4, the total cost of the meal must be 4x3=$12. Eight dishes have been eaten. Each one costs $12 ÷ 8 = $1.50.

Melanie brought 5 x 1.5 = $7.50 worth of food. Her share being $4, she receives $3.50. Cam brought 3 x 1.5 + $4.50 worth of food and receives $0.50 .

CECIL'S CHAINS

Cecil leaves 10 small chains intact and opens 9 links of the last 3. With these 9 links he connects the first 10 chains. To close the link chain, he only has to open and close a last link. So, Cecil opens and closes 10 links, which is done in: 10 x (10+4) = 140 minutes.

TAXI TWINS

25 minutes after starting, Rickie finishes the first lap and Mickie has only driven 25/30 of the circuit, or 5/6. So, Rickie gains 1/6 lap on Mickie every 25 minutes. He laps Mickie in 6 x 25 minutes = 150 minutes, that is, 2 1/2 hours.

SILLY 7s
$(7 + 7 + 7) \div 7 = 3$
$[(7 \times 7) + 7] \div 7 = 8$
$7 + 7 - (7 \div 7) = 13$
$(7 \div 7) + 7 + 7 = 15$
$(7 \times 7) - (7 \div 7) = 48$
$[7 + (7 \div 7)] \times 7 = 56$
$[(7 + 7) \times 7] + 7 = 105$

PAGE 24/25
PROFESSOR McMATH

The answer is always 1,089.

A MATH GENIUS

1. 55   3. 190
2. 210   4. 155

PAGE 26/27
MATH MAGIC

If there are only 3 digits in the number you get the last 2 digits give you the day of your birthday and the first gives you the month of your birth.

PAGE 28/29
A TEXAN OUTSMARTS THE BANDITS

There may have been only 1 nugget in the bag. When the Texan took 1 leaving zero the bandits would each be left with nothing. Probably, the bag held 61 nuggets, which is the smallest multiple of 2, 3, 4, 5 and 6, 60, plus 1. But there may have been any multiple of 60 (plus one for the Texan), e.g. 61, 121, 181, 241, etc.

LETTERS TO CAMP

The father's problem comes out to

$$\begin{array}{r} 715 \\ +9511 \\ \hline 10226 \end{array}$$

Did you catch Bill's father's trick? He could not have sealed the envelope when he wrote the P.S. or he would not have been able to enclose the letter.

QUICK QUESTION

The answer is 2. Here's how to work it out:

$\frac{1}{2}$ of 2 = 1 $1 \div \frac{1}{2} = 1 \times 2 = 2$